Pax and Blue

Lori Richmond

A Paula Wiseman Book
SIMON & SCHUSTER BOOKS FOR YOUNG READERS
New York   London   Toronto   Sydney   New Delhi

For Cooper and Holden, with love.
May you always be there for each other—
as brothers and friends.

SIMON & SCHUSTER BOOKS FOR YOUNG READERS
An imprint of Simon & Schuster Children's Publishing Division
1230 Avenue of the Americas, New York, New York 10020
Copyright © 2017 by Lori Richmond
All rights reserved, including the right of reproduction in whole or in part in any form.
SIMON & SCHUSTER BOOKS FOR YOUNG READERS is a trademark of Simon & Schuster, Inc.
For information about special discounts for bulk purchases, please contact Simon & Schuster Special Sales at 1-866-506-1949 or business@simonandschuster.com.
The Simon & Schuster Speakers Bureau can bring authors to your live event. For more information or to book an event, contact the Simon & Schuster Speakers Bureau at 1-866-248-3049 or visit our website at www.simonspeakers.com.
Book design by Krista Vossen
The text for this book was set in Sentinel.
The illustrations for this book were rendered in ink, watercolor, and charcoal, and composited digitally.
Manufactured in China
1116 SCP
First Edition
2 4 6 8 10 9 7 5 3 1
CIP data for this book is available from the Library of Congress.
ISBN 978-1-4814-5132-1 (hardcover)
ISBN 978-1-4814-5133-8 (eBook)

Some kids have a dog or a cat or a fish.
Pax has a pigeon he calls Blue.

"How are you today?" asked Pax.
Blue answered back.

Pax knew it wasn't so easy being little, so
every morning he brought a bit of toast
and shared it with Blue.

But this morning was different.
Pax knew little ones can get rushed along—
especially when Mom can't be late.

Blue didn't understand.

And there was no one to explain.

Poor Blue, thought Pax. *I left him alone . . .*

in such a fast and busy place.

And you don't leave a friend behind.

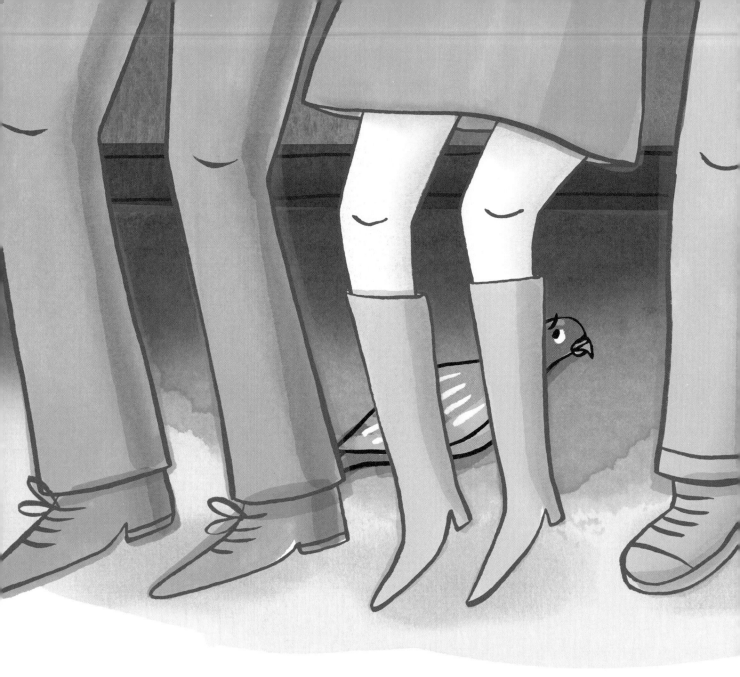

But Blue wasn't left behind . . .

Blue was lost, and didn't know the way out.

Uh

oh.

Oh no!

Blue had no idea what to do.

But Pax did.

"I'll help you," said Pax.

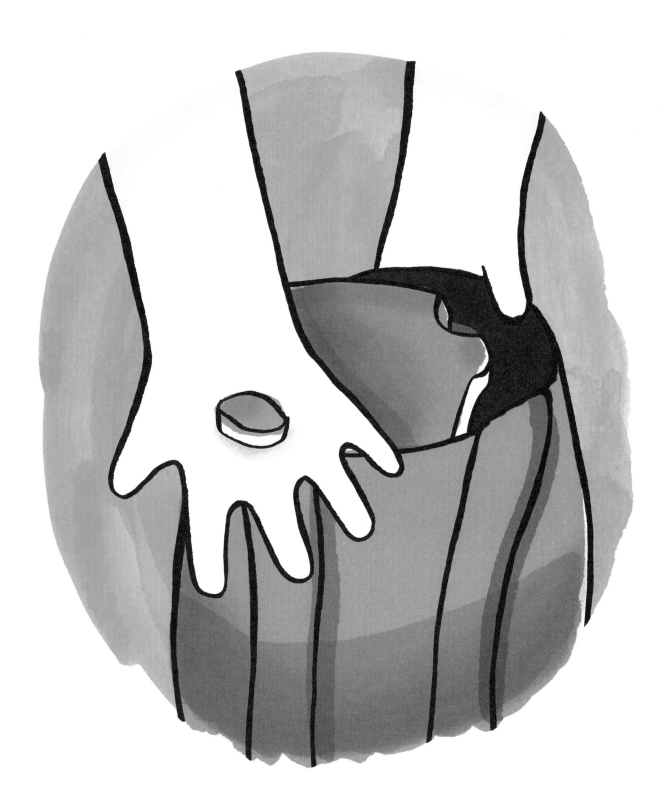

He knew . . .

just what his friend needed.

And Pax knew . . .

he would see Blue again tomorrow morning.